THE NIGHT WATCH NINJAS

Lily Roscoe • Lisa & Damien Barlow

Lon... New Delhi

These are the Night Watch Ninjas.

Their job is to keep your town safe
from evil night-time mischief.

Their numero uno most wanted
bad guy of the year is:

STINKER THE STINK-MEISTER SMELLYKINS SKUNK

POLICE DEPT
50522

(also known as Sir Smells-a-lot,
Pee-Yewsville, Yucky Pants
Stench Master the Third).

He may look cute, but underneath that bushy tail is

THE BOTTOM OF TOXIC DESTRUCTION.

Here are the ninjas, enjoying their usual midnight feast, when suddenly ...

NEWS FLASH!
STINKER THE STINK-MEISTER HAS ESCAPED FROM PRISON.

THIS IS A CODE RED SITUATION.

The ninjas' tasty snack turns into a crisis meeting!
But just as they are planning their first move . . .

...Stinker drops one of his atomic mega-bombs of

STAAAAANK.

"CAN . . .

NOT . . .

BREATHE,"

gasps Possum.

"WE'VE LOST HIM TO THE STINK!"
cries Grandmaster Fox.

There's no time to lose. The remaining ninjas must stop
Stinker before he smothers the world with evil stench!

"QUICK, NINJAS," says Fox,
"TO THE WARRIOR WAGON."

They cruise the streets, searching for Stinker.
Through her binoculars Koala spies a large
green cloud erupting from the cinema.

NIGHT OWL SCREEN

BAT CAVE CAFE

"It must be another stink bomb," she shouts.
"Ninjas, to the Night Owl Screen, NOW!"

The ninjas bravely investigate the pitch-black room.
Mole deftly detects the weapon's location.

"**STAND BACK,**" he warns,

"**IT'S** A . . . A . . .

... a piece of stinky old **CHEESE?**"

Clearly this is one of Stinker's sneaky tricks.
"Where IS that no-good skunk?" cries Mole.

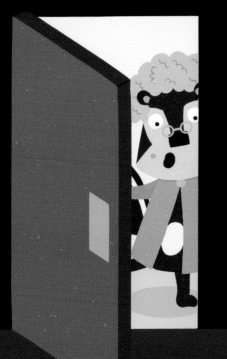

"Excuse me, sir," calls a little old lady outside,

"I just saw that smelly Stink-Meister run into the Bat Cave Cafe."

"NINJAS," says Mole, "TO THE BAT CAVE!"

They enter the cafe,
but quickly realise
their mistake ...

"Wait – who just
locked the door?"
asks Koala.

"Why is that skunk dressed as
a little old lady?" asks Fox.

"IT'S A TRAP!!!!!"

But just as all hope seems lost...

...a hero descends from the heavens.

"POSSUM, YOU'RE ALIVE! IT'S A MIRACLE!" cheers Fox.

The Night Watch Ninjas are reunited.
It's time to catch that evil skunk once and for all!

"NINJAS, HOLD ON TO YOUR NOSES, WE'RE HEADING TO SKUNKSVILLE!" says Fox.

SKUNKS VILLE

With her night-vision spyglasses,
Koala spots Stinker heading for . . .

. . . the all-night supermarket.

SKUNK-O-MART

BEANS →

But the place is enormous
and full of SKUNKS!

Luckily, Fox remembers an important ninja rule.

"A true ninja must get inside the mind of the opponent," he says.

"What does Stinker love? What does Stinker crave?"

"Bananas?" says Possum.

"Bagels?" asks Mole.

"Butter?" suggests Koala.

And then it hits them . . .

"STINKER LOVES BEANS!"

The ninjas dash straight for the bean aisle . . .

"Call the coppers, Possum!" says Grandmaster Fox.

"This stinky butt is going back behind bars where it belongs."

"That's what you think," sniggers Stinker.
"Nobody puts the Stink-Meister in a cage . . .

To Teddy, Walter and Nate, my very own Night Watch Ninjas – L.R.

To my brother, Brandon – D.B. & L.B.

Would you like to be an OFFICIAL MEMBER of the

NIGHT WATCH NINJA CLUB?

All you need to do is pass this very difficult test.

Can you . . .

pat the top of your head four times while saying,
"NINJA NINJA NINJA NINJA NINJA,"
really really fast?

And can you . . .

master the world-famous KRAZY KOALA AIR-KICK?

And can you . . .

make this sound in your very best ninja voice?

HAAAAAAWAAAACHAAAOOOOO!

CONGRATULATIONS!

You are now a member of the Night Watch Ninjas!

SIMON & SCHUSTER

First published in Great Britain in 2018 by Simon & Schuster UK Ltd, 1st Floor, 222 Gray's Inn Road, London, WC1X 8HB
A CBS Company • Text copyright © 2018 Lily Roscoe • Illustrations copyright © 2018 Lisa and Damien Barlow
The right of Lily Roscoe and Lisa and Damien Barlow to be identified as the author and illustrators of this work has been asserted
by them in accordance with the Copyright, Designs and Patents Act, 1988 • All rights reserved, including the right of reproduction in
whole or in part in any form • A CIP catalogue record for this book is available from the British Library upon request.
978-1-4711-6467-5 (PB) • 978-1-4711-6469-9 (eBook) • Printed in China • 10 9 8 7 6 5 4 3 2 1